To Lauri and Lily

Dial Books for Young Readers
An imprint of Penguin Random House LLC, New York

First published in the United States of America by Dial Books for Young
Readers, an imprint of Penguin Random House LLC, 2022

Copyright © 2022 by Tao Nyeu

Library of Congress Cataloging-in-Publication Data is available.

Manufactured in China • ISBN 9780525428701
10 9 8 7 6 5 4 3 2 1
TOPL

Design by Lily Malcom • Text set in Fiesole and ITC Zemke Hand Com

The artwork was silkscreened with water-based ink.

The Legend of
IRON PURL

Tao Nyeu

Dial Books for Young Readers

Nobody could spin a yarn like Granny Fuzz. The children of the village could listen to her for hours.

"One of the greatest rivalries of all time was between Iron Purl and Bandit Bob. He liked trouble and she did not. It all began with the Batty Berry Bust . . ."

The bats came unexpectedly that day. They gobbled up every berry in sight, making a huge mess.

What brought them here? Was it another one of Bandit Bob's pranks?

The frightened villagers didn't know what to do. Those hungry bats didn't stop . . .

. . . until they heard a strange sound.

And then . . .

. . . they started seeing stars.

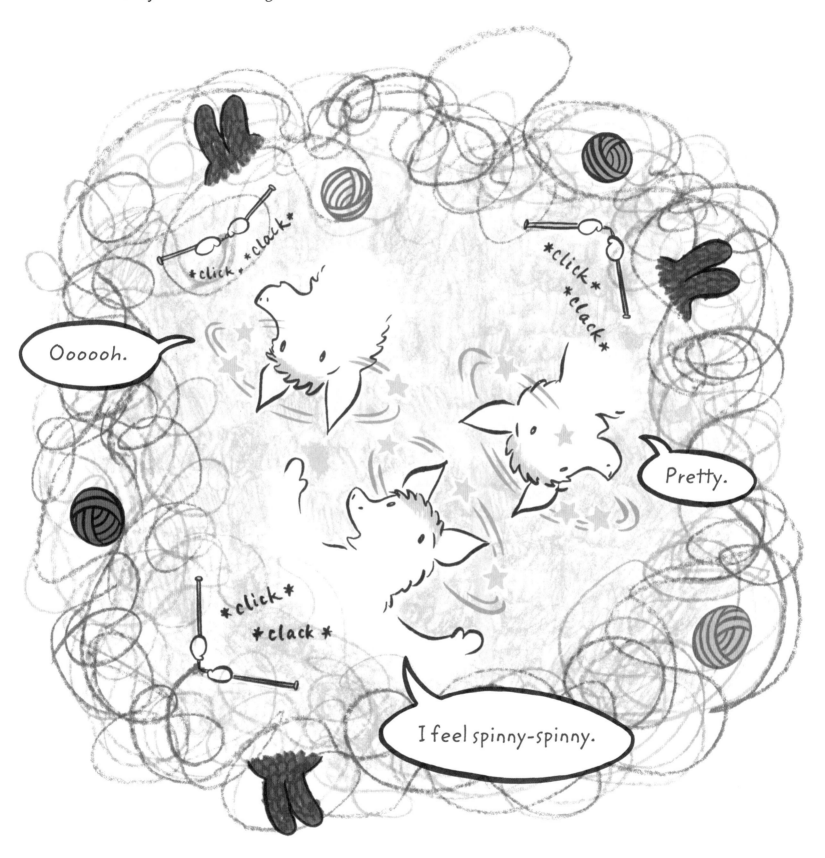

Before they knew it . . .

. . . they'd been knitted into tight cocoons, so cozy that they were lulled into a deep, delicious nap.

The mysterious knitter didn't stick around. But she left a letter.

What a grand idea. The bats loved it!

They apologized and cleaned up their mess. Then they planted a wonderful fruit farm. There were enough berries for everyone!

Iron Purl had ruined Bandit Bob's fun. Who was this strange newcomer?

"From then on, whatever trouble Bandit Bob
stirred up, Iron Purl always found a way to fix it.
Even when he caused trouble by accident, like
the Flaming Fairground Fiasco . . ."

The carnival was in town, and everyone came to enjoy the fun.

Unfortunately, a spark went astray.

Suddenly a fire broke out.

"Help!" cried the villagers. And then . . .

Hooray! The flames were being extinguished! But how? By whom?

The air was filled with the clicking
sound of knitting needles in action.

That could only mean one thing.

Iron
Purl

had come
to the rescue!

The villagers jumped safely down into Iron Purl's knitted net as the fire brigade arrived. Everything was going to be okay.

But wait! A cry for help! Someone was still in trouble!

Without a moment to lose, Iron Purl swung into action, shooting her trusty ball of yarn into the air.

Was Iron Purl too late?

Never! It was another daring save by Iron Purl!

Following the most important rule of fire safety, Iron Purl immediately stopped,

dropped,

and rolled.

The fire was out. Everyone was safe. Iron Purl was a hero, and Bandit Bob was jealous.

"How did Iron Purl always show up in the nick of time?"
"How did she have so much yarn?"
"Did Bandit Bob ever outwit her?" the children asked.

"Iron Purl had a solution to just about any problem.
It drove him bananas," said Granny.

He liked to steal pies.

He would snatch socks,

Why am I always missing one sock?

He would scare people with puppets.

—RAR!

AAAH!

So Iron Purl protected them.

and Iron Purl had an idea for that too.

And Iron Purl made them not-so-scary.

That was the last straw. Bandit Bob challenged Iron Purl to a duel.

Needles clashed. A lot of yarn was thrown.

It was the longest, most intense knit-off in history. Iron Purl was getting tired. She didn't know how much longer she could keep up the fight.

The next thing Iron Purl knew, Bandit Bob had her needles and was knitting her up in her own signature move: the Cozy Cocoon—enhanced with fancy cable work!

But Iron Purl wasn't going down without a fight. She noticed a loose end in his scarf. At the very least, she could unravel it. Nobody likes to be chilly!

She pulled hard on that loose end, and her yarn-winding reflexes kicked in. Faster than she'd ever been before, she wound and wound and wound. Bandit Bob began to unravel!

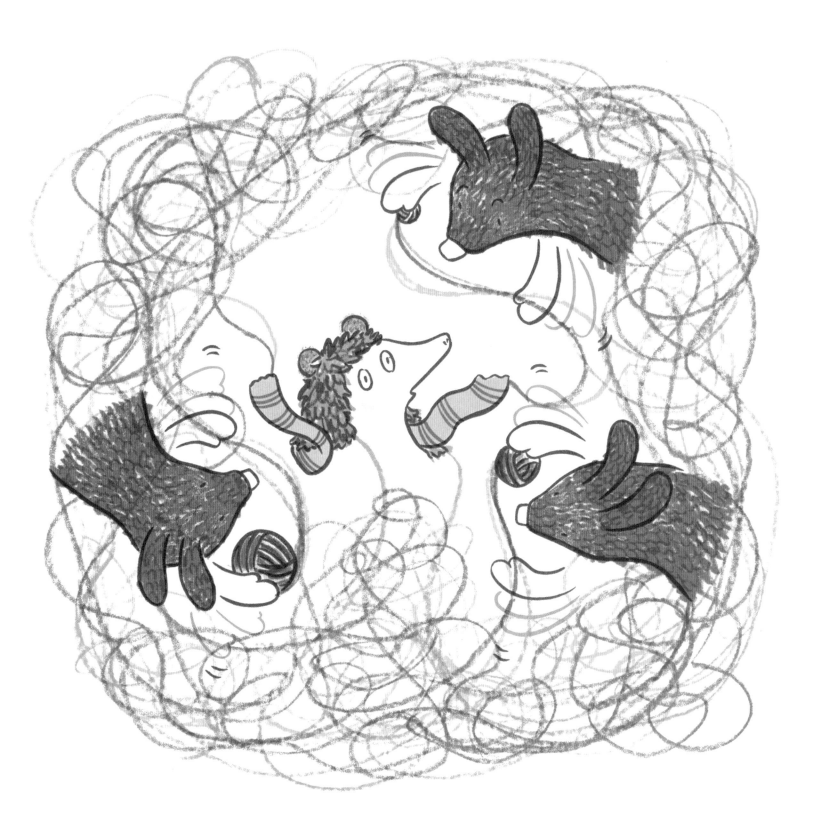

This wasn't just a scarf, it was a disguise!

Bandit Bob was not who he appeared to be. Not at all.

Undone and exposed, Bandit Bob confessed to everything. He was alone and lonely.
He knitted to pass the time. He made trouble to get attention. And his name wasn't Bob.

Something stirred in Iron Purl's heart. She understood, because being a hero with a secret identity was also very lonely. No one truly knew who she was.

Bandit Bob and Iron Purl
joined forces. The village
became safer . . .

LIBRARY

BOOK
DROP

. . . and much cozier.

But Bandit Bob had a mischievous streak that was hard to curb.

"And then what happened?" the children asked.

"*And then* is a story for another day," said Granny Fuzz.

It was time for the children to head to their homes for supper.

Thanks for the sweater. My mom loves that the elbows never wear out.

On their way home, the children talked about Granny's marvelous stories.
She had a way of making Iron Purl feel so real.

So real that even Granny and Grandpa Fuzz
were now inspired to go out for a swing.

Wheeeeeeee!

But the legend couldn't
possibly be true.
Could it?